Cris Casagrande

Letters to Somebody (I Used to Know)

WeBook Publishing - English Edition

Published by WeBook Publishing – Los Angeles, CA
All rights in the English language reserved.

This book is a work of fiction based on real feelings. The book explores the words left unsaid—the unspoken emotions, the memories tucked away, and the feelings that linger long after people have come and gone. With honesty and heartfelt introspection, the author invites readers into the complexities of relationships, self-discovery, and the quiet power of writing down what we can't bring ourselves to voice aloud.

For information, please email info@webookpublishing.com

First English Edition
Paperback
ISBN: 978-1-966892-04-5
LCCN: 2025901727
Written by Cris Casagrande
Translator: Daniel Moreira Safadi
Editor: Ana Silvani
Cover Design: Daniel Leite Fernandes
Illustrations: Ana Carolline Guimarães da Silva Dourado
Interior Formatting: WeBook Publishing

Manufactured in the United States of America.

"Never ignore your feelings.
I didn't ignore mine, and they may reach your eyes and,
who knows, even your heart."
- Cris Casagrande

Table of Contents

PREFACE

It is not uncommon for something to be left unsaid. Be it for fear of hurting someone, lack of courage, a decision to preserve the peaceful stability of the room, or just because the feelings are not yet sufficiently developed at that moment.

Sometimes, we don't know what to say, and sometimes, we don't know how to say it.

Some unload their feelings in punches, screams, kicks, and arguments; some do it through some sort of art, and some keep their feelings shut in a voiceless chest, marked by regret. All these people have something to say, something bellowing within their throats that, for some reason, has not been properly said.

I always keep a stack of paper in the first drawer of my nightstand, which might have been a gift, an old schedule, or a cute little notebook that I bought for $1.99. In these pieces of paper, I keep my feelings, my unspoken words, which end up written in whatever way they find most appropriate.

My own mother complains that I don't go out much, so in the practical world, I may not have lived much (yet… or not, I don't know; one knows nothing about the future), but I have already lived a lot in my chest and in my head. (Un)Fortunately, none of this has reached my throat, but it has at least reached the paper.

Many people have crossed my life, people who come and go, as they should. Some of them I follow from afar. People I knew well, I knew with my heart, to whom I dedicated words, the true activity of my vocal cords. Today, I know only a tiny part, the memories they have of me. They have barely become acquaintances. There are those I wouldn't greet on the street.

My throat has left many things untold to them, but my questionable handwriting wrote letters addressed to my drawer. Now, these words may not even fit anymore (after all, you don't go after that Junior High classmate with a genius comeback you thought of after the fight was over), but they are still manifestations of feelings. Some serve me better, including some of which I laugh at when recalling the past. Past is past. One does not return to it but checks the documents.

Remember, there's no need to say it out loud; you have your reasons, and I understand that. But never ignore your feelings. I didn't ignore mine, and from my fingers, they may reach your eyes and, who knows, even your heart. This letter I dedicated to thee, and here are some that were dedicated to other people: (former) friends, (almost) lovers, and faces of myself which I insisted on knowing, the hardest (un)known person to decipher.

Cris Casagrande

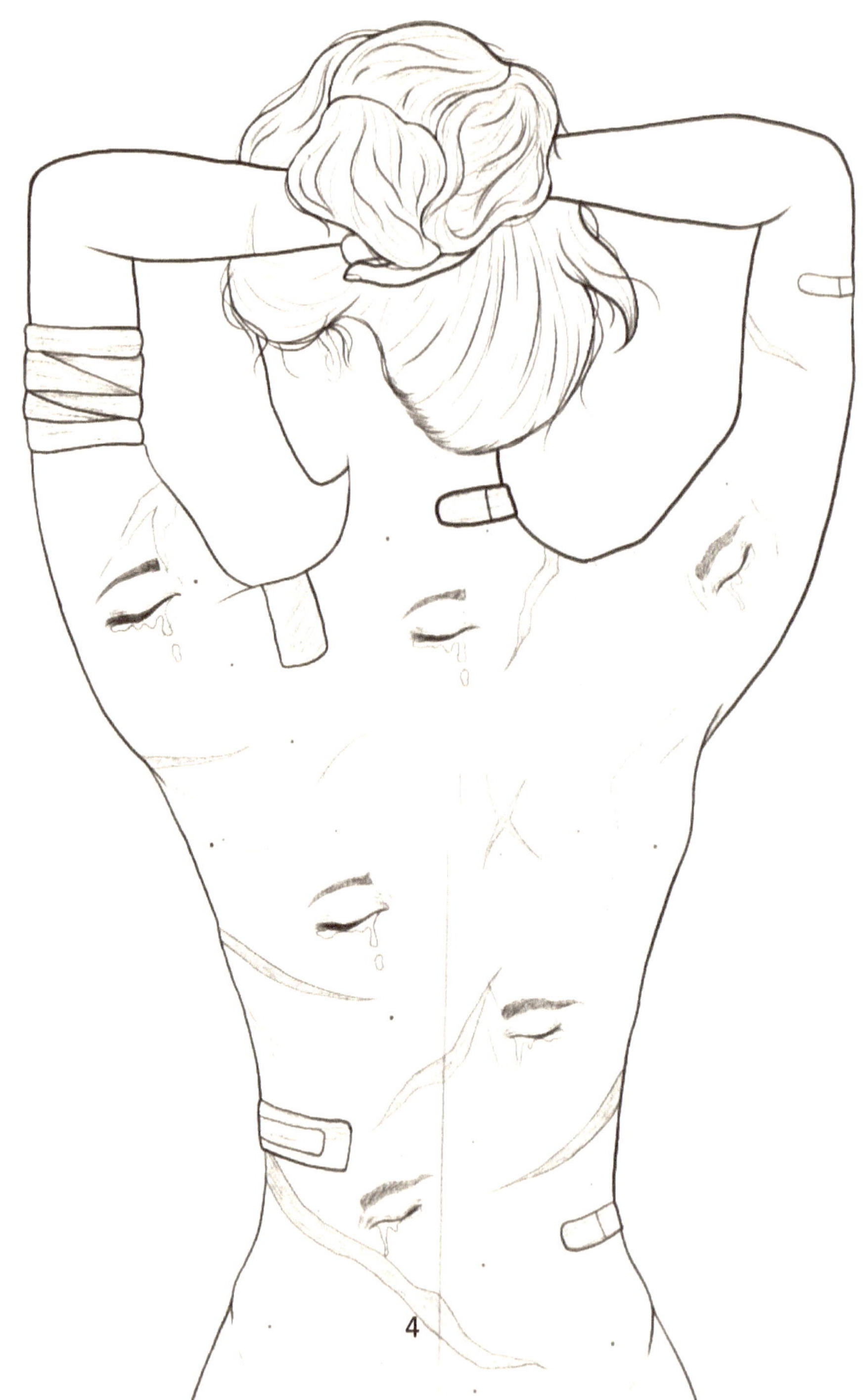

FIRST PART:

To Those Who Hurt Me

I

I don't think I can handle
Another "love" story
Always with the same pattern
You have no idea how much it hurts
When devotion becomes indifference
When I keep trying to save
Whatever's left between us
While I relive our first kisses
My selective memory
Made-up plans I made for us
Made-up expectations I promised not to have
Made-up safety I allowed myself into
Not anymore
It hurts too much
While I'm ready to call it love
You call it nothing

II

I promise
I'll be quiet
Next time
I'm overcome with tears and screams
I dreamt with my own despair
And while I slept
I wished to awaken no one
I don't want them to mind
The voices in my mind
Nor the cry that hurts my head and my throat
All may hold their peace
They deserve their rest
I promise to shrink
To hold my own warmth
And quietly
I slept again

III

I don't know whom I'm asking
But please stop
With these grueling dreams
That hurt my throat
Because no one hears me
I even speak, scream actually
But all is ignored
For nothing is real when I awake
In the remaining time
It is so real
It even hurts

IV

9

I learned to count on more than the disillusion
While you declared yourself to someone else
Said standing by you was so complicated
That was just for me, you forgot to mention it
I've apologized for the chains
Didn't learn to escape the claws
Of what you can't even call love
I'm going there, promise I won't be
This source of sorrow by sunset
I'm going there

V

You lied to me
I believed it when you said it'd all be well
That my pain was more than just a drop
In a sea of lost people
You lied
And things didn't change
I still believe you
I know nowhere else to look
If I look at myself
I lose myself even more
It shouldn't be this way
You lied to me

VI

Incredibly long songs annoy me
Maybe they don't move me as much
Or maybe it's just my generation
Weak
Unfocused
Talking about problems
And caring for their minds
To avoid getting insane and stray
Weak?
Insane and stray
But not weak
Surviving through memes
And songs… but not too long
They have the right time
Just like each of us
A weak mind?
Surrenders and becomes addicted
A strong mind tries again
As much as it hurts
And it's going to hurt more
And the pain, almost numbing, is not quite addictive
Because it would all be so much easier without it
Maybe it would be easier if I were weak
And suffered at once
But here I am
Listening to a long song
And getting a bit less annoyed than yesterday

VII

Come back
I miss you
How pathetic
I don't want to waste ink on this
Don't come back
It wouldn't work
If I were to work
I only resurrect you when I want to feel a spark
Of what was once love
As I don't feel anything else

Bye
Don't read, don't listen
Not worth it
Just… go
Again

VIII

13

I promise not to love you anew
I promise to lose your face amidst many or few

IX

If you saw me today
You'd find my hair short
My gaze deeper
And my tongue fainter
But if you saw me today
You'd find my hair long
My smile a bit fake
And my shirts loose
"Hey, how you doin'"?
"Good, good. I'm… great"
That's the answer you'd both get

X

15

I was told I spoke too loud
So I shut
I was told I was rude
So I shut
And held myself to avoid another mistake

Shut it, voice in my head!

XI

What have I done
To you?
Don't know
But I can't be close
To what you did to me
Is my bliss annoying?
Is my talent disparaging?
You don't even know how unpleasant
Your shallow comments are
The problem is you
Don't even have a name
And it still hurts me
Anonymously

XII

17

If a voluble being
Suffers to lie
They fail to see
The empty value
Of their statement

XIII

I stopped singing
Don't really know
I think I stopped singing

I stopped singing
Don't know if because of them
But I stopped singing

I used to sing along
To show I was happy
And now all is quiet to me

It's easier to blame the others
Am I really to blame? Is it just them?
I don't know

All I know is I'm losing my voice
LOSING MY VOICE
I let them take it away

And stopped singing

XIV

That was me
Not sure it's her
But it wasn't
And it had been me
And even when it wasn't
She wasn't also
I swear I tried
I struggled
Damn it!
I'm tired of giving up
That's not me

Not to my true self, my best self; I liked her so much; come back to me, please.

XV

I may even do a little
But I still can do more
And turn this hoarse scream
Into a mix of (tuned) vocals

XVI

I've become indifferent
Like you
No
I'd be lying if I said that
There's still empathy in me
An unaffectionate one
I've become realistic
Mocking hope
Listening to jazz
I guess I've become a grumpy old man
But on good days
I become a Tumblr girl
Reading poetry is good
Writing too
Living this life
Maybe not so much

XVII

You said
"I never forgot that day"
"Sometimes I'd catch myself thinking of you"
"Please, I need to see you again"
And the worst of all
"You can believe me"
I believed
Wanted to see you again
Kept thinking about you all the time
Remembered that day
And then I ended up in tears
Because of what you did
The texts you didn't read
And refused calls
I didn't get it
And to this day I can't get it

XVIII

23

From you
I just want that part of me
The pieces you took
Even aware
That, without you
I wouldn't be this way that I am today

Fitting what I once was
What clung to your body
With my own now
Mended, frail, with missing parts
For I gave in too much
And the pieces may not even recognize one another

XIX

I miss you
A lot, you know?
I don't even care if this is beautiful
Well-written
Subjective
And so poetic it affects
Because now I'll be corny
And say you affected me
And I was almost stable
When I remember my prince
Full of flaws

Incredibly real
I miss you so much
I hide
From almost all people
This sleeping princess
Who really wants a love story
And is there quiet
Awaiting for the time to wake
Maybe with a true-love kiss
To love back
And stop pretending
"No love"
Lie, do love
And pull me along
So we can love us
And long
And miss

Call me
Text me
Tell me…
I won't start preaching to myself
About how I need to stop suffering
And what love is… that's all
It hasn't been cracked yet (could you do it?)
I only came to say I miss you

XX

I
You
Jasmine
Park
Anavitória
Laid on the grass
Looking at the sky
You kiss me
Just don't wake me, ok?
You don't wake me, ok?
Just kiss me
Looking at the grass
Laid on the sky
Victory on the park
You in jasmines
I
Confused, or my confused dreams
I was confused and awoke

XXI

There are things we know we won't know
before we find out we are no longer part of what
was

Some heartaches eat us up inside and
won't be cracked by those who crave meaning

There is you
There is me
There is that that never was
There is the story that didn't happen
Of what we could be
There is our kiss by the lake, which was unbelievable, I tell
you
There is last week and the next, when we won't meet
There is the night
There is the awakening
Thinking of you with chills
There is what aches
What you take and the little that is left
In the completely empty period

XXII

Flow
Let it flow
Flow
A volcano

Stop
Stop it now
Stop
Stop for you

A way
A one-way
Your way
Every day

Failed
A failed act
I failed
Every day

XXIII

I promise I will
Find life incredible
The problem-solving journey
Fun and possible
I promise tomorrow
I won't lose it
Nor give it all up
Mistaking screaming for crying
I promise tomorrow I'll learn
To be a new me
Accept and follow
The path I was given
Tomorrow will be better
Tomorrow I'll only smile
I promise
Tomorrow I'll fulfill
No lying or quitting
I'll make you proud
But now I'm only trying to exist
So tell my mind to be quiet

XXIV

Cardiac dismantle
An ammonia mine
Celiac girl
Stuck in rite
To sicken, to strengthen

Breathing carbon monoxide
Avoiding hydrogen sulfide
On the way to her throne,
A water reservoir
To meager, to plead

Aesthetic of ugliness
Holds hands with a warm caretaker
Who takes the harness
To hear the sufferer
Who'll bliss, who'll bear

XXV

31

Truth is I'm too weak for this world
No one's done this to me
I simply am
No point in pointing the finger
The problem is I don't know the solution
I've tried to leave
And always came back
I've been here for so long
My countenance has changed
And my hugs have ended
I wanted to take this weakness out of me
Or simply being taken out of it

XXVI

32

I'm embarrassed to confess
That I wanted to mark myself
Or intoxicate… anything
That would carry me away
To see them blaming themselves
Not for any specific thing I can mention
Even because I won't hand in the information that easily
You beat yourself up figuring it out
Thinking about what detail you missed
Regretting whatever

I'm even more embarrassed to confess
That this wish isn't fully gone

XXVII

I had my eyebrows done
Because I wanted a pretty goodbye
I colored my lips
To be appreciated from above
Bathed in condolences
And late apologies
I dyed my hair
To be thus remembered: Beautiful
Before smudging the mascara
Before smudging the lipstick
Before smudging my whole body

XXVIII

Ten minutes seeding
Refuge to allure
My eyes were red with so much crying

Twenty seconds remembering
The birth of weep
The crazy confusion caused the slip

An hour thinking
Of that old coat
Which one shouldn't rest upon

Four days walking
Heart throbbing
With nowhere to go

One month sinking
Seeking a place
Where it would be safe not to breathe

Time has stopped
But nothing's left
Nothing

Television activism

XXIX

35

My selective memory
Wrecks me
It reminds me of good kisses
Pretty laughs
And memorable flavors
Throws to the background
The fact that these memories
Are full of people
Who don't deserve to be remembered

XXX

I know what came easy
But no one knows
Of the times hidden in the closet
Of the screams in the bedroom
Until I felt like puking
Of the objects cut
The ones with faces
To feel that "death"
Soothes me
To see myself wreck
And not wrecked
I know what I hear
And see in the gaze
I know my own fear
Of not deserving
To get where I want to get

XXXI

I wanted something real
A post-carnival thing
Spend March diving in the salt
But in January, things weren't well already
I had so many plans for April
I forgot that where we come from,
It's around this time that it turns cold

XXXII

You hurt me
Corner of the mouth
Innocent eye
Open indifference
With few words
Or none at all
A laugh
Meant to be whispered in my ear
It blurred my memories of you
The loving hug and care
Shattering prejudice by knowing you as a listener
With an innocent eye and a laugh in the corner of your
mouth
It's all over
In a whisper
Of your ignorance
You hurt me

XXXIII

39

What's the harm in saying what you feel
When you're not here
What's the harm in saying what you want?
Since I'm not a psychic
Just needy
Just woman

XXXIV

It's even ridiculous how much we match
Our contemplative way
With childish laughter
That laughs at the same things
Likes the same music
And fits a hug…
But you don't care
And I tried, more than once
I waited for you,
I bent
Looked for you to start over
But you don't care
And I don't want to suffer again
Seeing you admit your mistakes
Apologize
But never change
I'm done with clinging to the good times
I value them, and I was happy
But you have chosen
And I choose to care for myself
And for my aching chest
I won't cry this time
I'll just carry on
Maybe I'll dream of you
Maybe I'll still write thinking of you
But with the clear conscience
Of one who has tried

And I respect your choice
I'll withdraw
Please withdraw as well
From my chest and my head
So that I don't cry this time
I insist
On not suffering for your choices
It would be ridiculous

XXXV

42

And now I started thinking of you
Just because you said no
(After two months saying yes)
It's nothing but a bruised ego
It's even embarrassing
I don't know what happened
All I know, strangely
Is that time may pass
We always end up bumping into each other
We've been like this for about nine years

XXXVI

You pull me
And your eyes repel me
Your fragrance pulls me
And your words repel me
Your hands pull me
And my mind repels you
My wanting pulls you
And my fear repels you
Your being pulls me
And your voice repels me
Your kiss pulls me
And your ideas repel me
Your affection pulls me
And your questions repel me
Your touch pulls me
And my questions repel you
My singing pulls you
And your complications repel me
My wishes pull you
And my thoughts repel you
Your heart pulls me
And you repel me

XXXVII

Going and coming
And never breaking away
The center goes underneath
And soon wraps itself around the cord
And this cord chokes the center
And it flees for freedom
But soon comes back again
For it can't be away from the comfort of the thread
And they fight and make up
And the inches of their dimensions entwine
And they wear out
Of this going and coming
The thread wears out
And worn out, so worn out that it'll break

You said we were like a yo-yo
While playing with the lighter you were going to use to light
your cigarette

XXXVIII

I'm used to it already
To being heartbroken by you
You're a crush
A memory
A wish to go back in time
A wish to have you
This ache means nothing
It doesn't even ache
It's not even an ache
After I found love
And the ache it can bring
You've become just… just this
It's easier to have my heart broken by you
It's cozier
It's funnier
Than by him
Who wrecks me
Drives me to pieces
Drives me to despair

XXXIX

46

And intolerance killed another one of your relationships
If we can call it that
Your extremist manner
Your incisive manner
Kicked me out of your arms
The way you think you're better than the others
Such a shame
I liked your smile so much
Drowned in dimples
I liked your smell so much
I liked the smile that followed
A stolen kiss
But now I look at you
And only view void
Such a shame
I was enjoying our story
Of us liking us
And leaving the differences aside
But you chose to praise them
Offend me
Reject me
Break me
Such a shame

XL

47

My body asks for you
But the rush of my heart
Freaks me out
For the warmth of your hug
Is not cozy
Is not safe
Is not for resting on your chest
And listening as if it were the sea

XLI

I don't see you as human anymore
You see me as a tool
And I see you as a worm

I still dream of you
Of the other versions I made of you
Of the good memories my unconscious kept

Lately, I've needed to get away
Outrageous and painful as this, which is
The last poem I write thinking of you

XLII

49

Life can if it isn't cut
Life fades if you fail to water it
Life remains unknown if it's not nurtured

XLIII

Call me
By a name only you know
Call me with gestures
With the subtlety of your look
Call me
To go out
To stay in
Now
Call me now
Call me
And don't let it cool down
Just call me
No need to explain
Just because you want closer
Because you need a moment
A hug
A caress
Noodles
I'll try and solve it
But call me
Don't forget
And call me

XLIV

51

Nobody takes a chance
Everybody follows the music
Just how the piano calls for it
And I listen
I feel
And then I see
Too many prints together
The corny pants, like pajamas
The bleached hair (which isn't good)
The imperfect movement

And I stopped being perfect
The day I was born

XLV

I wanted it no longer
These falling days
When the glazed eye is beautiful
And pain is something
It's feeling something
It's feeling a lot for no reason
It's wanting to vanish
Without knowing how to explain
It's not knowing love
It's finding oneself
In an ocean of losses
It's wishing to shave the head
To tear off the skin
And stuffing some sense into that brain
Or just take it off
Seeing it fly
Away
While the chest falls
Closer to the feet

XLVI

It's been some time
And what do I want with this passage?
The beginning of the weekend?
New years of life?
See him…
If he remembers to text me at noon

I had never cried in anger
I had never wished for myself as I do now
Being what they sing, I say and can't
Kissing in the rain
Without remembering yesterday
Repeating mistakes tomorrow

XLVII

54

Were you surprised when you were told?
Maybe even shocked.
What did you think?
I, nothing.

Did you find it bullshit? Bad?
Did you think I was wrong?
Did you feel sorry for me?
I, myself, found nothing.

What I did.
You called it bitter.
I was unhappy
But now I think I'm nothing else.

SECOND PART:

To Those Who Didn't Know Me At All

XLVIII

58

Only God knows
Why I find myself beautiful as I cry
There is something charming
In my tears
But just mine
I never liked the sadness of others
Something inside me
Likes to see me suffer

XLIX

Who knows, today's the day
Of a chat with those who see me from above
I feel good
And I don't feel bad for feeling good
I know what I'll do tomorrow
But not in five years
And this doesn't scare me that much any longer
I've had moments of true joy today
On such a beautiful and common day
In which I didn't love my lunch
Nor the book I'm reading
I didn't even produce anything
But… ok
This is what I asked for at the last cathedral I visited (or nearly)
I don't have all my meds
Injections, healthcare professionals
And the countless interventions, clinical or not
I don't like the expenses of it
And always end the day small
Without understanding so much
And liking it
Remembering it's ok not to know
What's out there
What comes next
And I just left my bubble
But I didn't burst it

And I remain around
Because life is what it is
Things are what they are
And I am what I am

In movement (micro, which is better than nothing)
Changing just what is up to me
Getting a little less desperate
And remembering to thank

L

You don't have to smile just because you took off your
braces
You don't have to go out there finding new red flags
Because there are too many already
So many people whisper about it
Without knowing your crosses
Avoiding the lights
To hide the bad intentions
That ignore your paths, your constellations

LI

62

Lips that never screamed are sealed
Unloved children don't know the word 'no'
Tongues gossip here and there
Dancing between mouths

LII

I've already been marked
By some sketchy stories
By a foul mouth
Who dared to kiss me
With poison in his teeth
Poison in my marks
I saw life dry up
In the skin of my back
Before it was cleaned
But not fully
The marks aren't mine
They were granted to me
By some disaffection
And lovelessness
Then, I created my own
I was the one to grant them
And those, I may try
But won't let go

LIII

64

I wonder
I wander
Wondering for so long
I wander
Wander where?
To the waltz
I waltz here
I waltz there
What waltz?
A dance?
A waltz
I wondering
And writing
This awkward thing
To a waltz
Nobody understood
Not even me

LIV

65

Out of a chance
I made two
And chose the two of them!
For I learned with the first
And was happy with the second

LV

I don't want to make these verses sad
This is a declaration of love after all
They should be a bit better
Since they have loads of love
They turned out this way
Because this love is unrequited

LVI

I'd like to know how to rhyme
I really, truly wanted to
But as I don't know what to try…
I'll leave that up to you

LVII

How long does it take
To be able to do it again
What has been done already
Once more
How long does it take
To go back in time
And fly through the mind
As we did
And how long does it take
To see with my eyes
What I don't even know
If I hope and wait
And how long does it last
This time
That confuses me so
Looking from the outside
If it was the time
If it was my time
Well, I don't know
All I know is I regret
Not surrendering
The new solitude
Doesn't seem fair
But holds tight
To try and explain
And they laugh and yell for so long
Always thinking
It's all so slow

LVIII

69

I learned to love
I learned to wait
I learned to discern
I learned to learn

LIX

I get involved
And I got involved again
With another story
I got into it
Fought with it
Cried for it
Joy
Fantasy
It gave me
Wish I were
The master of this story
Living deep
In a conversation
In an action
In an illusion
So fake
But so real
To me
So ideal

LX

I made them understand me
In a funny way
Without truth
I made myself a doll
A lunatic in a dress
I made myself senseless
So I wouldn't need to find some
I made myself goldless
So I wouldn't need to have some

LXI

I made myself small and make myself insignificant
Don't think I'll do something important
Let it get lost at once on the lips of itinerants!
Let it be less in this decaying environment

I am pretty small but not insignificant
I still don't know if I'll do something important
But that's fine, as long as it shall enchant
With a small trace

LXII

73

I wanted to listen without hearing
I was silly, dropping and leaving
I let prostration consume me
I let cowardice take over me

LXIII

Freckles all over my body
Freckles forming constellations
They are everywhere
My arms, legs, back
Marking me
Showing me
Identifying me
They are mine
There's a bit of me
In my freckles
My little marks
Birthmarks, life marks

LXIV

75

I'm nothing
Nothing more than I can be
I live on my path
Looking for you
I am nothing
Nothing more than I just am
I know I'm nothing
And follow I still will

LXV

You know
I feel I'm not alone enough
But I feel a little lonely
When I want to withdraw surveillance
And start abundance
Of… everything
Today, I think I'm ready for the world
I think…
When we may leave home again
I'll leave the house

Spoiler: I didn't.

LXVI

I can't write anymore
I can't smile anymore
Then, I learn and unlearn again
I can't stand this repetition anymore
Going back and forth with no break
I don't want anybody reading it and feeling sorry
I want my animal instinct
To stop disliking life
And just keep it
I can't stand my bed's humidity anymore
And my disappointment in myself
And with all the things that are

(This is ridiculous, I know
But, as I said
I can't write anymore)

LXVII

Once upon a time
There was a cat
And other stories I wasn't told
Before bedtime
I wasn't told
That people disappoint
That loving hurts
That the wind wounds
That falling down is routine
And standing up too
Maybe I was even told
But I, a child with sparkling eyes
Chose to ignore
And learn for myself
So that later
I could tell my next stories
About people who disappoint
Love that hurts
Winds that wounded
Letters that weren't sent
Between caresses through the hair
Pecks and blessings
And turning off the lamp
I dreamt of Cinderella
Of Snow White
And of my own princess story
Which became routine

Falling down and standing up
A never-ending once-upon-a-time
A Cheshire cat a million times
Want me to tell you one more time?

LXVIII

I had some very crazy parties
Slumber parties
With myself
In my bed
Closed eyes sometimes
Just for a change
My head
Staged a revolution
The biggest I've ever seen
It hit my heart
But got lost in the way
Misled by loneliness

LXIX

81

I have nothing to smear today
I forgot how to sing today
I decided to lie down today
When reality gets out of my way

LXX

Did I put the sheets of paper to good use?
Whatever
I could have made a little boat
Or a plane
To see it fly away
Through navigation
With something a bit better
Than these poorly written words
Do what you want with them
They aren't even mine anymore
I threw them out
And throw them out!
They're all yours… Enjoy!
If you think it's the right thing to do
Smear the ink
Rubber it
Cross it
Forget
You didn't put the sheets of paper
To good use as well

LXXI

I thought he and I were the perfect match
Stillness in the storm
Comma is the period
It hurt
This exclaimed end
At times interrogated
And not well-ended
And I thought it was a sheer ellipsis
That I had to go back to have some coherence
Then I saw I could match someone else
The twilight stillness
The kiss and… the longer kiss
Then came stillness and perdition
And finally, stillness and retardation
I let it pass and he got lost
It hurt the other time
But it passed
As it always does in the end
If it was the end
For who decides when this story ends?
Where I'll fit in my stillness…
Maybe in a song
Caution, ambition
Maybe even stress, loneliness
(Just to make it clear, I hope not these last ones)
And go matching
Placing commas

Semicolons when pauses are longer
And colons to explain better
And my everlasting ellipsis
That will only cease
When the Universe no longer is
I match myself well
Stillness to stillness
Beauty to beauty
Day to day
Castle to castle
Dragged to fit in
A little brick that fell
Will be there, on the floor
Not everything fits perfectly
But still matches
Mixes and rhymes

LXXII

I write little
I do little
I feel little
The poet is barely sane
I feel little
I do little
I write little
But I've actually gone insane
I don't even write
I don't even do
I don't even feel
I just repeat myself
I don't even feel
I don't even do
I don't even write
Disappointing and losing my own poet

LXXII

Time is a healer
A silent appeaser
It blurs the pain
And makes love plain

It's a massive killer
A service to linger
But always efficient
In preventing the same grievance

Kill me, kill you, kill her
The skill of a born sufferer
Boss, friend, father, mother

Rid us slowly of this danger
Turn and twist to the last drop
In the end, time made it stop

LXXIII

Should I say I want a love?
I can't say
If I want a love to hold
But I don't seek an object
To my love devote
If that is possible
I must be told
That there's a way
To love without aim
Not relying on reciprocity
Not being a hostage to longing
Not seeking in humanity
A loving hug
Box of chocolates and flowers
All clichés for now I forego
All male names I let go
I want just love, no blushing
No suffering, just loving
If someone knows a way
Tell me right away

LXXIV

A morning hoping to study
An apple slushy
A strong chewing gum, pepperminty
A croissant, just a bit, truly
Wearing a shirt, it's woolly
It belonged to my cousin
I live in memories
Where I dreamt of the future
I live in the past
Holding to what is for sure
Longing will never be gone
I won't even cover half or one
In the van, music is playing
Playing games with Jean
Playing the game of life with my sister
Down the slide, true enrapture

LXXV

Disturbance
Disturbs the ache
Turbulent, perennial
And then
Calmly formal
Close to amid
You mint
That the ensuing
Is potent ache
Perturbance

LXXVI

I don't feel happy
But I have pink kitten slippers

I have a dog feeling sick
A cold week on the way
Papers to hand in
Loneliness sneaking in
Sweating at night
While feeling cold
A piercing that started to hurt
And a career that is very uncertain

I don't feel happy
But I saw a beautiful movie
I petted my little one
Had tea
And put on my pink kitten slippers

Maybe happiness needs to be built on small things

LXXVII

I want to belong only to myself
The image of a free girl
I don't want to be the apple of his eyes
I don't need to be a muse either
I can be adored today
And forgotten tomorrow
When I'll cross new streets
And become a bit more myself
My own
Dancing on the paving stone
Pretending to fall in love
(Wish I knew how…)
Memorizing details for fun
Being myself
Drawing looks
That are not mine
Just being my own
Walking alone
And being enough

LXXVIII

Tell me
A pretty boy
With whitened teeth
Who seems shallow
And big-headed
But I have so little love to give
That I want no exchange
In any (dry) well
Then he called my attention
I don't recognize this sort of attraction
But still melancholy
This I know well
From other times
Not good times, with joy or praise
Just a dance
That ends like this:
"…and now I'll start to
Blow illusion bubbles"

LXXIX

(What is to follow is nothing more than declarations to a stranger)

I'd love a mocktail
Kiss me
That's the name of the mix
No alcohol
With alcohol, it's called kissed
Concrete, concluded,
Done, realized
Bold people
Too drunk, too determined
Carnal lips
Seeking a prey
And us…
Partisans of extreme consent
Who remember all that happened last night
We kill romance
And surprise
Drive fearlessly
No roses in the glove compartment
Or madness in the blood
Just one more day
Running through the same streets
Praying to avoid any accidents
And who knows, go head on
Into the rest of our lives

Made of cocktails
Well-dressed people
And tattered dancers
To the sound of nothing
Kissing in the rain
And I, afraid of catching a cold
Running in the desert
Swimming on the ice
Finding gold
Burying despair
And here I write
While I wait for you
To invite me for another drink
(No alcohol, I'm driving)

LXXX

I didn't want to write sad things
Running, away
Always late
In happiness too
Put off to tomorrow
But I can't pretend

I've written a lot of gloomy things
That might even be beautiful
Asking for an epilogue
Full of curves ending the letters
Because they were true
I can't pretend

When I miss something
It's from ages ago
From a time of illusions
Faith, grace, and peace
But I can't write about that
Because I can't pretend

LXXXI

I'll read a letter
Telling your story
I'll shed a tear
Touched and tired
Aware of the years
Scars and passions
Quivers and anxieties
When this is all over
Keep it, remember to tell
Remember to recall
Remember to live
All this I'll read one day

LXXXII

The supreme in the mouth
An absent-minded whistle
An unsteady step
Arms loose by my lap
The taste of a popsicle in the summer
And chocolate in the winter
A party treat
And a kiss on the cheek
(Maybe not, but I wanted this lame rhyme)
Is a stillness juice
Singing your favorite song
Laughing during the day
And drooling while napping
Screaming in anger
Enjoying the silence
And some other emotions
Are a moving statement
In the corner, softly
That you're happy

LXXXIII

98

There are some things I regret
Some pictures I didn't take
Some things I didn't say
Drinks I didn't taste
And times I did forsake
But they're gone
And if they're gone
Today I take new blurred pictures
Say new bullshit
Drink new bitter drinks
And live new disappointments
We're always in "what if"
Thinking that which wasn't
Would be the best in the world
But have you stopped to think
That you're living your best version right now?

LXXXIV

99

Once
I let the ink run
In dark tones
Feeling it burn
Is that the purpose?
And I look at the mark
I know it's not eternal
It's just something to remember
That life changes
While we let it down

LXXXV

Tell me
How to take my hair off
Of the pillow
My blond little tips
Are glued to the slip
Because the brown roots
Pull it from the inside
… nothing…
There's nothing to pull

LXXXVI

I need to know what time it is
Without control, I'm not myself
Without control, there's no tomorrow
Without control, tomorrow comes
Without control
Without control, the gas runs out
Without control, the water dries up
The well is dry, thirst is up
Without control you can't take a test
Come, don't control answers the without
Without control, all turns into a mess
A play turns into a plush
Fragile and inflammable
Terrible, unimaginable
Without control, I lose myself
Without control, I wish
To control myself
Just control
Control
Without control, I'm not myself
I need to know what time it is

LXXXVII

Why do I miss something
I can't even name?
My heart snaps
My mind cries
My whole body screams
Before shutting down
It asks to shut down
To stop feeling
This cruel lack of something

LXXXVIII

They call me Blabbermouth
They forget words are my life
Without them, I'm nothing
Without them, I don't write
I don't read, I don't sing
I don't speak
If I fail to speak
They come from my head to my eyes
Trying to reach the mouth
Wishing to leave, to exercise
The blabbermouth loves them
But fears them too
For just a misplaced one
Is enough to destroy her

LXXXIX

Go
Take me elsewhere
Go
Take me where?
Go
TellmesomedaythingswillmakesenseandIwillstopfeelingindan-
gerallthetimewhileIgatheredstrengthtocallyouIforgottobreathe
Don't go!

XC

I don't want someone complicated
With a database of concepts
Phrases and effects
(And, not of, don't mix it up)
Who tries to change the world
And in constant reaffirmation
I want things to be easy
Without the need for effects
With naturality
Without even needing to remember being
Who makes me forget the world
While affirming
Anything stupid and/or irrelevant
(And/or to increase the possibilities)
Someone like me
Who just tries to care about nothing

XCI

You know?
I don't know
I thought I felt sure
Comfort
I confess
I got it wrong
I feel the same as before
But for no reason.

I don't usually use a period
But I did
For no reason

XCII

I like this feeling
The energy flowing out
I feel so bohemian
Overcome with serenity
Little by little
I'm not morbid
I don't see beauty in any wandering
Except mine
Which is just potential
Because in tears
I confess I want to be vital
Walking caffeine
Annoying, nobody can stand
But if I manage to be happy
Nothing else matters

XCIII

I don't see the Sunlight
I feel the Sunlight
Through the light of my eyes
In the light of your eyes
Everything reflects
I'll call someone
To read these reflexes
Complex and with a complex
More than your own being

XCIV

I dance to sad songs
In front of the mirror
Led by the melody
And by the feeling that invades me
I forget there's more out there
And I remember to be just me
Away from the concepts
Of those who would find these steps weird
Feeling nearly complete
I don't want anybody to find
I don't want anybody to dismantle
My utopic solitude

XCV

Another thing I haven't done
Another time I have lost
Another life to be gone by
Another nothing-but-forgettable day
Another disappointed sigh
Same feeling of guilt and want
Static
In a landscape I don't like
But don't change

XCVI

Want to know me?
Here are a few things I love:

I love remembering where and how I was when I read a certain book
I love breathing the air of a museum and feeling transported
I love feeling the true love of my dogs
I love laughing at the things I did, said, or thought when I was a teenager
I love it when I can stop thinking (and it's rare)
I love feeling the Sun on my body
I love making my family laugh
I love feeling a melody leading my true movements
I love feeling the smell of corn (although I hate eating it)
I love singing loud or really low for my appreciation
I love knowing dialogues from series and movies by heart
I love singing in the car
I love seeing Jasmine's silly joy
I love seeing photo albums
I love my ability to feel touched when remembering
I love realizing my evolution
I love it when he makes me feel like the only one in the world
I love forgetting my age
I love having lunch at the cinema
I love the feeling a country house brings me
I love *Nono Balin's* strawberry ice cream

I love the feeling of completed tasks
I love hearing the sound of the sea
I love feeling connected to someone
I love slow and soft kisses
I love forgetting the whole world and staying in my private
little world
I love making up cute scenarios for us (even if it is just fic-
tion)
I love feeling pretty
I love remembering the way only I do
I love physical memories
I love feeling a different way (although it hurts sometimes, I
wouldn't live without it)
I love seeing a melody flow through my fingers
I love my love for the world of entertainment
I love my waist
I love my bunch of freckles
I love the end of a productive day
I love chocolate and strawberry pizza
I love waking up and seeing the episode of some TV series

There are a lot of things I hate too
But leave it to another time

XCVII

Would you have time to listen?
To read me, in my angst
I've asked for time to stop
Today, I ask it to run
And take me to a time
When the time is mine
And I decide
What is done with my time
I let time be time
The rain falls, the Sun shines
The clock spins
The hands point
To me
Master of my own time

XCVIII

114

I'm not tied to anyone
But I tie myself up to images of the past
This melodrama tires me
Drains me
Distorts me
And I feel like writing sad words
Even if I don't want this
I lose myself inside of me
And despite these feelings
That don't abandon me
That don't leave me alone
So, I give in and write

XCIX

115

Hit the head on the wall
Rest on the hammock
Between one jump and another
I lose myself and my breath
I convince myself that I'll never again leave this in me
I think it's all wrong
And a part of the fault is mine
I go to sleep and wake up lighter
I slap my conscience
I remember to forget to try to please everyone
I displease
I dissolve
In my desolation

C

Seven days are so few
For those who need a month
One life is too long
If you only take one risk
Serpentine is trash
For those who don't like Carnival
One person is all
If they make you feel special
"Tell her she's beautiful, and don't forget to say…"
Singing and dancing under the moonlight, feeling the smell of
rain and the lightness of feet

CI

Have you seen the sky today?
Have you noticed the movement of the clouds
Dissolving a turtle
To become a strawberry cake?
Have you taken a deep breath today?
Feeling the smell of caramel
Mixed with the dew
With that weird chill
Touching the nostrils from the inside
Have you seen yourself today?
Thinking of everything you are
Of the child who ate sand
And wore Snoopy socks
Of the impatient teenager
With no parties to go
Of the adult you've become
Or are becoming
Have you passed this energy on
To the dogs in the way
The flowering blossoming
And the humans nearly gone?
Don't let any particle become a memory
Before giving it it's due importance

CII

Do you know when you feel lost?
When all was faith
Decisions and certainties
Turn into paper boats
That spread through the sea
And that my little feet
An unprepared girl's feet
Can't reach
Lingers the sand trail
Like a mermaid's tail
Taking shape around me
Saying, "Hey, and now?"
"You, don't take long!"
"Take us to play around"
And my feet dance
With the whys
Wander, balance
Drawing on the soil
Jump and tap
Without moving
Stuck with one another
Afraid of walking ahead
Ashamed of walking back

CIII

Sitting on the sidewalk
With a devastated face
A man asks me what day it is
I say it's Tuesday
And my tap is clogged all the way
I bought so much detergent
But now it's indifferent
Because all will be sitting in the cupboard
The kitchen is brand new
My voice is in tune
But I still don't know if I know how to sing
I can't cook anything fancy
And what made sense is now history
For the mind hops restlessly
I don't particularly love cauliflower
He doesn't call me love at any hour
The rest of the sidewalk is empty
It's so cold my hands are frosty
I should go home

CIV

I don't like the new so much,
but keeping the mistake pleases me
That's why I expect the new start anxiously

CV

121

Touch me
Very carefully
I don't want to be anybody else's
Or even nobody else's
Just mine
Married to my thoughts
Absorbed in trembling eyebrows
Another one whispering in my ear
"I want you"
Me too
I want me

CVI

I'm an expert
In drowning
In memories
Clinging to the past
Laughing at what hurt
Tickling on the nose
Tucking hair locks behind the ears
While I smile at the memory
Of the images before me
Clinging might not be the right word
Because I was
Today I'm dazzled
Charmed by my own story
Which comes poking
At the corners of my mind

A whistle calls me
"Wanna know the future?"
No, thanks
I'm good here
Feeling the present

CVII

123

We've lowered it to 10 mg
So what I wanted was 0
Not 15
Which is when things don't make sense
Nor 30
Which is when things don't even exist

CVIII

Those days
Inner rain days
With thunder, noises, and riots
Days when getting up
Is painful
Days when the smile
Is untruthful

My good thoughts
Fleeing away steadily
Flinging into the wind jointly
Parting slowly

Wordless
Fallacious
A precious part of me

125

PART THREE:

To Myself

CIX

I can see
You doing things thinking of yourself
I can see
You feeling less guilty
For not owing anyone anything
I can see
You are not thinking of changing the world
Just thinking of improving yourself
I can see it
And I'm proud of you

CX

I want something more
To say
The problem is I just repeat myself
In this dissatisfaction routine
I hear the noise of the rain
And remember, tomorrow it starts again
Is it ok if we skip a few years forward?
Just to be sure
Just to know if I left the places I didn't like
And overcame
This wish to say more

CXI

You've always been inside, haven't you?
Latent pangs in specific moments of my childhood
Afraid
But that's ok, it's your essence
I don't know who you are
But I know you've suffered a lot
And I promise it'll all be ok
I'll heal us both
And you shall be able to rest
And I shall be able to blossom
And feel just the power
Mine, which I still don't know
And yours, which could finally leave

CXII

Can I rest on you?
Maybe only after I learn to rest on myself
Not afraid of the dark
Not feeling that almost painful stretch
I imagine a million things for us
For us to live
On simplicity and foolishness
But fearing excessive childishness
I took the bonsai screen off
And want to see myself grow fast, free
Will you water me?
Just like that song
"Because dying of love is a joke"
I'm tired of jokes
It's my time to fulfill (myself)

CXIII

132

It's Sunday evening
Whose taste is upsetting
It doesn't have to, it's ok
But I'm going to sleep feeling too small
The kind that needs a long-lasting hug
That contains my whole self
And it makes me feel it's ok
Together, we'll beat what makes me cold
And I'll feel warm within
Why don't I feel capable by myself?
I should be enough to myself
But I'm too small
To fill this void

CXIV

There's no reason
To fear the night
The Moon won't hurt us
Especially when I have
The Sun in my hands
The warmth always comes back
The light always comes back

CXV

Growing up doesn't have to be this bad
And it's not even because things are the way they are
But because we're managing to be happy
In a way, we haven't been for a long time
You know, since childhood
Which wasn't even that good at that phase, in-between
(But we pretend it was because we don't want it to get bor-
ing)
I don't want to promise because I'm not sure
What I have is a feeling
That sad and bad days are coming
While happiness will last a lifetime

CXVI

I brought you a cup of tea
For you to drink
And for you to know
That it'll be ok
And as you are me
You'd better believe
I know that things are cloudy
As much as your sight
And that listening to Elton John helps
But it's no solution
For this craving to call someone
So you don't feel lonely
But they don't pick up
They don't understand
And you get worse
So I brought you a cup of tea
For you to drink
And as you are me
You'd better drink it

CXVII

I took long
But I came along
He talks
I read…
And then I write!
To him and to me

I was stuck for some time
Tired
Or just lacking inspiration
Maybe it was too much for my heart
Or maybe I'm not even in love
It's just my nerve…
And illusions
Always an illusion
I imagine too much
And get too little
That's it, that's life

CXVIII

Let it go,
Let it be.
Let it flow…
Let it grow!

CXIX

You have nowhere to go
You have no reason to stay
And every time you repose
You'll get lost to explain

CXX

That I'm silenced
That I'm told what to do
That I shouldn't
That I should have
That I don't even know
That I don't follow
That they say
That they whisper
That, yes, they order
That I'll go
That I'm free
That I accept
That I believe
That… in what?

CXXI

Hi girl, calm down
Don't be like that, breathe
Green, yellow, red
Blue is soothing
Blue sky
Calm
Sun
Beautiful day
In the sky
With a veil
Made of Sun
Breathe girl
Calm down
Don't let yourself
Go
Don't let yourself get carried away
Breathe, girl
Blue
Ocean water
Calm down

CXXII

If someone stops to wonder about our existence
They will be shocked by life in an instant
Wondering how deep
Can one leap

(Verses with which I have dreamt. I woke up and wrote them down quickly, as fast as I could remember. I vaguely remember the dream. I remember there was a song I sang and more verses, but I can't tell you what message my self led by Morpheus intended to convey.)

CXXIII

(Selective memory)
Stop!
Let me think about him a little bit
About how I miss him
His hug
His kiss
His way
Of being immature with me
Of wanting everything with me
How I wanted not to want
Him, us together
We are so good together
And I've already shown you
I've told you
I know I feel more than I should
(Loser)
Damn it!
I'll go to sleep

CXXIV

Malleable position
With a censor's vision
Fear of an adventurous direction
And coerced affection

In your insanity
For rough reality
And the future battle
Is ripe, surprise, and adult

Which you aren't, green
No help in swearing
There's been a lot of mixing
In this girl so charming

There's no walling the wall
There's no cure for you at all
In this life of yours, full of stitches
Of pieces that need nurture

CXXV

Enough, daughter
Go to sleep
You're lost in your daydreams
Whole days in a stream
Here's Mother telling you
Go to sleep
I rest my hand on your head
Waiting for you to sleep
Only wishing you well
Little undeveloped adult
Don't forget to leave your coil
Don't be always spoiled
But forget until tomorrow
Because tomorrow, we'll see it through
And I still remember to take care of you
Enough, my daughter
Calm, rest, and try to let
All muscles to relax
Go to sleep

CXXVI

Take me far away
From here
But there is not enough
I miss
Mother's lap

CXXVII

Go
Go slow
You can't stand all this time without an airflow
Go
Go slow
There's so much onto you can hold

CXXVIII

Wishing to color my body
Red
Make abstract art
With deep strokes

CXXIX

I need a new love
It doesn't even need to be love
Just passion or admiration
To serve as inspiration
I don't write titles on my poems
Don't measure or make diagrams
I let myself feel in love
But not for someone…

CXXX

Don't lie about it
Just feel it
Admit it
Don't fight it

It's no shame
It just is
It's not a victory
It simply is

So let it be
Let it go
As I should be
Let it flow

CXXXI

He's always been honest with me
He just forgot to fall for me

CXXXII

Having the chance to give the first kiss
Walk in the park
Feel the rain
Be, somehow, free
Is sheer luck
Why is it this way?
With such a body?
In such a time?
Because it is this way,
With such a body,
And in such time
Without asking, be thankful
What can I ask when moving through
I have somewhere to go, legs to run
(And I think) still a lot from here on
I may be bothered by silly things
I may think I can change the world
I may run for a hug
I may do whatever there may be done
And it's nothing but luck

CXXXIII

It wasn't here where I wanted to be
Breathing deeply, I count the minutes to leave
But I know this is where I need to be now
So things may happen
I hate the stiffness I put myself in
And what these hours do with my day
But I know this part
Of what's going to be a part of me
I promise
I'll have looser limbs again
And one day, I'll have what I really need
What screams in my ears
What can't wait anymore
Your time will come
I promise

CXXXIV

What happened with my youth?
I don't remember living it
Having stories to relate
Loves to reckon
Achievements to crave
And systems to question
I don't know
I didn't do these things
And they say this is the youth
Maybe they are wrong
Or maybe I'm still too young to understand

CXXXV

154

When I write something decent
I'll call you
When I finally end what needs to be done
I'll call you
When I'm satisfied
Then I'll call you
Wait, where are you going?

CXXXVI

155

The sound of rain
I'm thinking of what I want and need to do
A literary hangover
And a damn emotional need
There's an alarm clock
Set to ring in a few hours
But I'll probably be late again
For now, I'll stay only with the sound of the rain
The expectation of a holiday next week
And the surprise that it is
On a Monday
To be feeling… well

CXXXVII

Loving
Myself
Seeing beauty where it isn't
Is it ignoring pain?

Loving
The ocean
Summer with the smell of sweetcorn
Or the immensity that may drown me?

Amen
And more
After the litany
Comes the restless night

CXXXVIII

I can't depend
On a "soul mate"
Or on a dream come true
To finally be happy
What if it never comes?
What if I can't make it?
Will I surrender, frustrated
 And try to hurt myself?
I can't even do it well
But I can feel at peace
Reading beside my dog
Watching a movie with a smoothie
Playing a game with my parents
There's so much I still want
There's so much I threw out
There's so much I need to learn
Like being happy now

CXXXIX

Thinking hurts
Because it never ends
It never answers what is always there:
Where did we come from?
Where will we go?
What are we doing here?

The goal is pretending you didn't see it
Getting lost in a new book
With your family about to start
And making up a universe of your own
To forget this one is nothing
Close to the real one

CXL

Wash your soul
With the weight of a constellation
With a children's song
And a passing benediction
Pull them closer
The hula hoop and the spinning top
A canary's song
A sorrel's gallop
A princess story
With a knight and a dragon
Crossing through the desert
In front of a pantheon
Wash your mind
With endless possibilities
The eyes of imagination
On cardboard facilities
From yellow to pink
That you saw on the screen

CXLI

We should like each other
But you're in the wrong hemisphere
I should be a museum wanderer
But I was born in the wrong century
We should not suffer
But then, no one could tell if we could be happy
A lot of things should be
She should have fallen on the grass
Not hit the head on the stone
But what can be done now?
I miss you so much
I'm still stuck in here
I don't know if I should move
But I don't care
It shouldn't be like this
I should have written something that made sense
But I believe I got lost

CXLII

Open the window
Let the sunshine in
Hear the cry of happiness
Trying to reach you

CXLIII

I'll give a beautiful message
I'll remember to encourage you
I'll be a blessed soul
Rich with joy
I'll remember

I'll walk by the cliff
Not afraid to fall
I'll run to the dawn
With no artifice
And learn to exist

I'll crown rebel hair locks
In love with your swing
I'll be energy, fully overturn
Felt on the skin
I will burn

CXLIV

A day which is mine
And it doesn't seem mine
For it rains
There's no "party"
There's no "present"
There's no trampoline
There's joy
There's presence
There's my bed
And there's more growth
Then you might think
Something else to do today?
Something else to be today?
No, today I'll just enjoy

CXLV

Am I living wrong?
Isolated, while the beach screams out there
And my chest screams in here
I'll censor myself when I leave
For not enjoying right
For not making more friends
Making up more love stories
I shrink in my bodily pains
In the farthest room of all
I wanted to be invited to something
But I don't even want to leave here
This is not right
It's nonsense and no good
This sentimental duality
That wrecks me

CXLVI

165

Aren't you tired of rolling on the mattress?
Fidgeting on the floor
Setting goals
And blaming yourself for seeing them forgotten?
This is the life I made
Empty promises
Inner battles
A desperate inertia
Salvation doesn't even have a name
But remains expected
I don't even cry anymore
I just resign
I yearn for a name given
The hunger has eaten

CXLVII

How can one be a person who feels such, so intensely
But who lives just as a bystander?
Outside, observing and reflecting
Seeing it happen
Longing for a moment of protagonism
I tell myself: "I'm sorry!"
And I'm in pain
It feels like it's all I can feel
There's no reason, no explanation
It feels like it has no solution

CXLVIII

It's good to be alone
Because alone nobody hurts you
You don't fall short of expectations
You almost forget the other in the world
Until you realize you're alone

CXLIX

Give in
This time,
Let go
Let it be
Stop trying to control everything
Learn
To bite what you can chew

What do I do while waiting?
Oh, if only I knew…

CL

The mind doesn't mind
Imploring and exploring
The words that flee
And fall
Hoping to see them flying out there
Wondering them elsewhere

CLI

170

Don't give away
Don't give in
Don't let them get you
Feeling something

CLII

Golden locks
Watered orbs
I got nearby
"Why do you cry?"
"The story's a sad illusion
A tale with no conclusion"
Eyelids close
Her locks rose
Told me, terrified
"The pain hasn't died"
"Please, no fears
Shed no tears
Tomorrow, you'll rise
And won't even recognize"
"It doesn't go away
An ill-being trait"
"Is it about who?"
"It's about you"

CLIII

I went back to my old writings
From years ago
From bad phases
From childish places
From what I now call practice
For a work I build

So good to see things have changed
Because I think they've changed for the best
And I (don't) even know myself
I see myself smiling
A countenance moving on
And hoping this will stay in the past

(But no haste)

ABOUT THE AUTHOR:

Cris Casagrande is a Brazilian author, singer-songwriter, and a graduate in Linguistics and Literature. Known for her intimate and heartfelt storytelling, she is the author of the YA romantic comedy trilogy, *Querida Alice, Carolina,* and *Para Cada Nome, Uma História.* Her newest release, *Letters to Somebody (I Used to Know)*, published by WeBook, marks her debut in poetry, offering readers a collection of personal reflections on love and everyday emotions that often remain unvoiced.

Casagrande's work creates deep, relatable experiences for her audience across both her literature and her music.

Scan to listen

These three original songs were created by the author as emotional companions to this book. Enjoy!